P9-DNP-822

Text copyright © 2012 by Emily Jenkins
Illustrations copyright © 2012 by G. Brian Karas

All rights reserved. Published in the United States by Schwartz & Wade Books,
an imprint of Random House Children's Books,
a division of Random House, Inc., New York.

Schwartz & Wade Books and the colophon are trademarks of Random House, Inc.
Visit us on the Web! randomhouse.com/kids

Educators and librarians, for a variety of teaching tools,
visit us at randomhouse.com/teachers

Library of Congress Cataloging-in-Publication Data
Jenkins, Emily. Lemonade in winter : a book about two kids counting money /
Emily Jenkins ; illustrated by G. Brian Karas. —1st ed. p. cm.
Summary: Pauline and her brother John-John set up a stand to sell lemonade,
limeade, and lemon-limeade one cold, wintry day,
then try to attract customers as Pauline adds up their earnings.
ISBN 978-0-375-85883-3 (trade) — ISBN 978-0-375-95883-0 (glb)
[1. Lemonade—Fiction. 2. Winter—Fiction. 3. Brothers and sisters—Fiction.
4. Addition—Fiction. 5. Moneymaking projects—Fiction.] I. Karas, G. Brian, ill.
II. Title. PZ7.J4134Lem 2012 [E]—dc22 2010024135

To: The Fabulous
Mrs. Mollo and
her fabulous
first graders!

And big thanks
to C.L. and T.H.
for sharing their
know-how
—G.B.K

For Ivy and
Daniel, who made
a lemonade stand
in February
—E.J.

The text of this book is set in New Aster.
The illustrations were rendered with brush and walnut ink on paper, colored in Photoshop, and finished with pencil.
Book design by Rachael Cole

MANUFACTURED IN CHINA
10 9 8 7 6 5 4 3
First Edition

Random House Children's Books supports the First Amendment and celebrates the right to read.

LEMONADE *in WINTER

A Book About Two Kids Counting Money

A SCHWARTZ AND WADE BOOK

written by
Emily Jenkins and
illustrated by
G. Brian Karas

An empty street.

Outside, a mean wind blows.

Icicles hang from the windowsills.

Inside, Pauline presses her nose to the frosted glass.

"I know!" she says.

"Let's have a lemonade stand."

Mom shakes her head.

"Nobody will be on the street," she says.

"Don't you see it's freezing?"

"We could *still* have a lemonade stand," cries Pauline,

skipping with her idea.

"Lemonade and limeade—and also lemon-limeade!"

Dad wrinkles his brow.

"Nobody will want cold drinks," he says. "Don't you hear the wind?"

But Pauline is jumping with her idea now.

"Lemonade and limeade—and also lemon-limeade!

Doesn't it sound yum?"

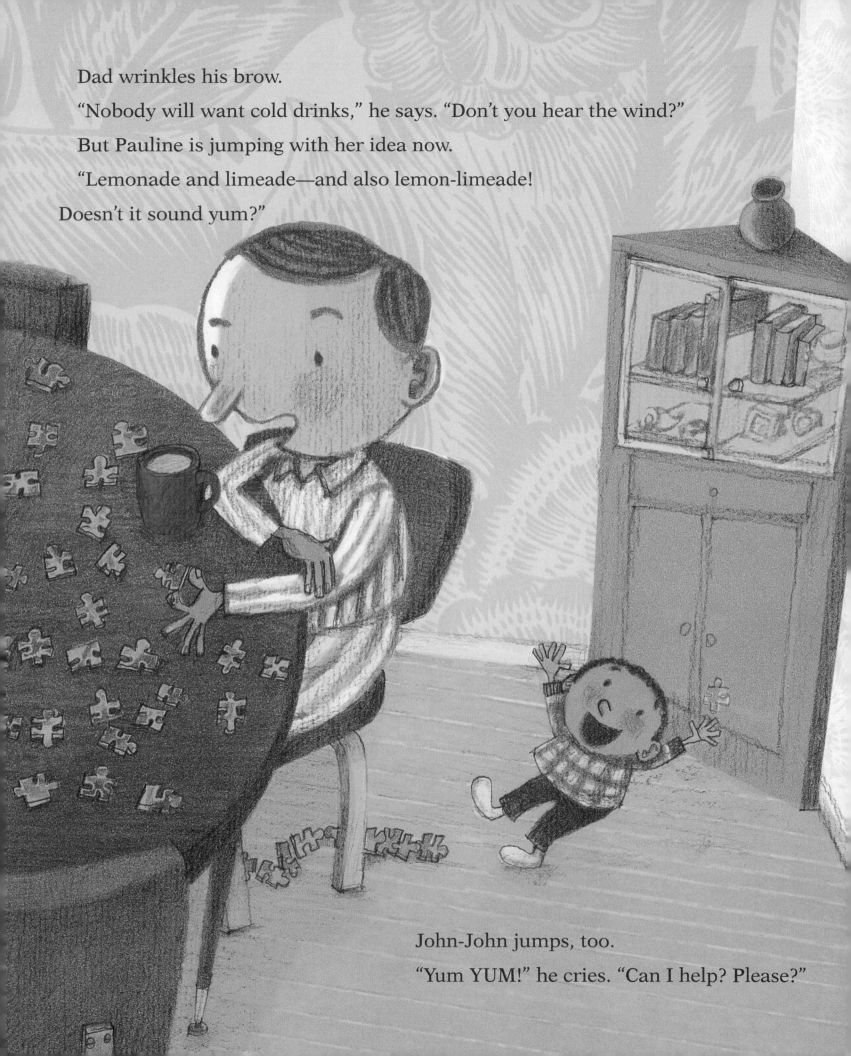

John-John jumps, too.

"Yum YUM!" he cries. "Can I help? Please?"

Pauline and John-John collect quarters.

They empty piggy banks and search pockets.

"Each time you get four quarters, that's a dollar," says Pauline.

"Four quarters, that's money!" says John-John.

Pauline and John-John at the corner store in hats and mittens.

Four lemons cost a dollar.

Four limes cost a dollar, too.

Two dollars for sugar.

Two dollars for cups.

"We have twenty-four quarters, and that's six dollars,"

Pauline tells John-John as she counts out the money.

They run through the bitter air with a large paper bag.

Mom says, "Nobody will be on the street."

Dad says, "Nobody will want cold drinks."

Pauline and John-John are too busy to hear.

Squeezing lemons.

Squeezing limes.

Measuring sugar.

Pouring water.

Lemonade and limeade—

and also lemon-limeade!

Outside, that mean wind blows.

Icicles hang from the windowsills.

"Maybe nobody *is* on the street," says Pauline, after a bit.

"Maybe nobody *will* want cold drinks."

"I'm on the street," says John-John. "I want them."

He grabs a cup of limeade.

"Don't drink too much," Pauline warns. "It's fifty cents a cup."

And still, an empty street.

Pauline thinks.

"Maybe we should advertise."

Shouting wildly, both together:

"Lemon lemon LIME, lemon LIMEADE!
Lemon lemon LIME, lemon LEMONADE!
All that it will cost ya? Fifty cents a cup!
All that it will cost ya? Fifty cents a cup!"

Harvey walks down the block with Milou, Mischa and Mungo.

"Cold drinks on a day like today?" he laughs. "Love it."

He pays, drinks a lemonade and takes a limeade back home.

"Fifty cents, that's two quarters," Pauline tells John-John.

"Two drinks is four quarters—and that's a dollar."

She puts the money in a green plastic box.

But after that, an empty street.
Pauline thinks.
"Maybe we need entertainment."
"I can cartwheel!" John-John leaps up.
"Good idea," she tells him. "I'll drum."

"Lemon lemon LIME,
lemon LIMEADE!
Lemon lemon LIME,
lemon LEMONADE!
All that it will cost ya?
Fifty cents a cup!
All that it will cost ya?
Fifty cents a cup!"

Ms. Gordon stops on her way into the building, holding Devon and Derek by the hands. "Let's see that cartwheel again, you," she says, a smile in her voice.

John-John cartwheels while Ms. Gordon buys three lemon-limeades.

Devon makes a sour face, but Derek drinks all of his.

"Remember, fifty cents, that's two quarters," Pauline tells John-John. "So three drinks is six quarters, and that's a dollar fifty." The money goes in the green plastic box.

But after that, the empty street.

Pauline thinks.

"Maybe we need to have a sale."

"Lemon lemon LIME,

lemon LIMEADE!

Lemon lemon LIME,

lemon LEMONADE!

All that it will cost ya?

Twenty-five a cup!

All that it will cost ya?

Twenty-five a cup!"

Aidan strolls up, arm in arm with Heather.

"Can I buy you a lemonade, gorgeous?" he asks her.

"Limeade," she says. "And yes, you can."

Aidan pays.

Heather kisses him.

"Twenty-five cents a cup now," Pauline tells John-John.

The money goes in the green plastic box.

But after that, the empty street.

Pauline thinks.

"Maybe we need decorations."

"Lemon lemon LIME,
lemon LIMEADE!
Lemon lemon LIME,
lemon LEMONADE!
All that it will cost ya?
Twenty-five a cup!
All that it will cost ya?
Twenty-five a cup!"

Rosa from the nail salon peeks out the door.

Then she calls her friends.

Five manicurists cross the street in puffy coats.

"Two limeades, two lemon, one lemon-lime, please," says Rosa.

"Five cups is five quarters, and that's a dollar twenty-five,"
Pauline tells John-John.

The money goes in the green plastic box.

Rosa calls over her shoulder as she heads back to her shop.

"You kids are crazy. You know that, right?"

At last, empty pitchers.

Pauline tips the green plastic box and pours their quarters onto the table.

Eleven cups sold.

Five cups for fifty cents is ten quarters.

Six cups for twenty-five cents is six quarters.

"Ten plus six is sixteen quarters, and that's four dollars," Pauline tells John-John.

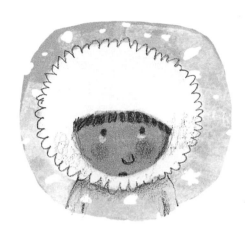

Then she begins to cry.

"Why are you sad?" John-John asks.

"We have sixteen quarters now," Pauline sniffs, "but we spent twenty-four."

"Sixteen is money!" says John-John.

"We didn't *make* money," she tells him. "We lost it."

"But look at all these quarters!" he shouts.

"Fewer than we had before," says Pauline.

John-John thinks. "Will sixteen quarters buy two Popsicles?"

Popsicles!

Two dollars each.

One lemon, one lime.

Sixteen quarters, and that's four dollars.

One brother, one sister.
One mean wind in winter.
One lemonade stand,
now closed for business.

LEMONADE
and
LIMEADE
and also
LEMON-LIMEADE

"Lemon lemon LIME,
lemon LIMEADE!
Lemon lemon LIME,
lemon LEMONADE!
Lemon lemon LIME!"

PAULINE EXPLAINS MONEY TO JOHN-JOHN

PENNIES are simple to pick out from other coins
because they're copper.

1 penny = 1 cent, easy peasy, lemon squeezy.
2 pennies = Well, that's just two pennies. Two cents.
3 pennies = Same thing. Three cents.

But:
5 pennies = 1 nickel. More about nickels later.
10 pennies = 1 dime. More about dimes later, too.
25 pennies = 1 quarter. Quarters are my favorite.
100 pennies = 100 cents, and that's a dollar.
See?

NICKELS are the most confusing of the coins.

They kind of look like quarters, but they're not.
I wish they were purple or something. It would be easier.
The thing to remember is that nickels have smooth edges.

1 nickel = 5 cents.
20 nickels = 100 cents, and that's a dollar.

DIMES are the cutest. They're tiny!

1 dime = 10 cents.
10 dimes = 100 cents, and that's a dollar.

QUARTERS are the best
and the biggest of the coins.

1 quarter = 25 cents.
4 quarters = 100 cents,
and that's a dollar.

DOLLARS are green paper.
They're worth 100 cents.
You can fold them up small
or roll them.

Don't rip them into little pieces,
because then they're no good
anymore.